Gorilla of My Dreams

by **Gail Rollo**

Illustrations by Mike Motz

Gorilla of My Dreams

by
Gail Rollo

Illustrations by Mike Motz

We sat in a movie,
My mommy and I.
It was kind of scary,
But I didn't cry.

A big gorilla
Came on the screen.
He was beating his chest
And acting real mean.

When we left the theatre,
While walking home,
I told Mommy I wanted
A gorilla of my own.

SCHOOL

We could play in the yard,
Swim in the pool,
And now that I'm five,
He could follow me to school.

That night in my room
I could actually see
A gorilla of my own
Was a possibility!

While snuggling in bed
It became very clear
If I closed my eyes tight
My gorilla would appear!

Falling asleep
I began to dream
Of a beautiful jungle
With mountains and streams.

Then suddenly I saw
A golden chair by a tree.
It looked like my size.
Was it there just for me?

The ground started shaking,
But I had no fear,
For I felt in my heart
My gorilla was near.

He is really BIG
Like I knew he would be,
And his eyes danced with love
At the sight of me.

Putting the chair to his chest
And his hand down to me,
He watched me climb in
Very carefully.

He lifted me up-up-up
To that beautiful chair.
It must have been magic,
For it just stuck right there.

We walked all around
As I squealed with delight.
I wasn't afraid,
But I still hung on tight.

I saw butterflies and flowers
And birds in the trees.
Is that a parrot
Looking at me?

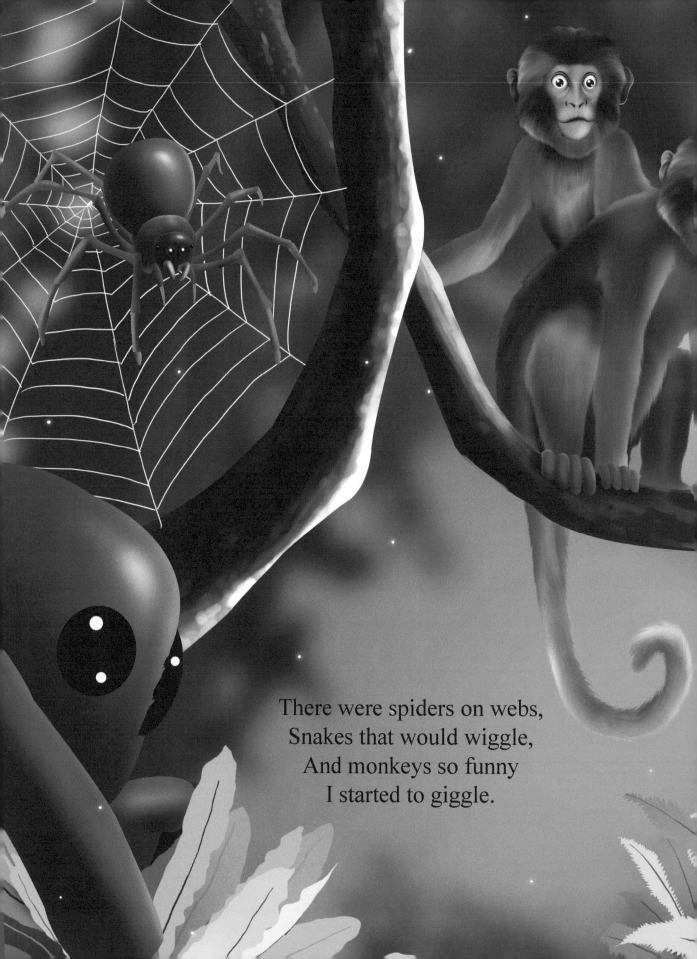

There were spiders on webs,
Snakes that would wiggle,
And monkeys so funny
I started to giggle.

He sat me down gently.
Then lowering his chin
He bowed down to me,
And I curtsied to him.

I started to dance
And twirl all around,
While he beat on his chest
And grunted real loud… BUT

When his hand hit the ground,
I flew up in the air!
But his other hand caught me,
Sitting me back in the chair.

He lay on the ground
With his face close to mine,
And we stared at each other
For a really long time.

Then I touched his face gently.
Looking deep in his eyes,
I told him I loved him,
Then to my surprise….

He leaned in real close,
And with a slight grin,
He whispered so softly,
"I'll see you again."

I woke up excited
To tell Mommy my dream
Of the jungle and mountains,
The caves and the streams.

Of course my gorilla
And the beautiful chair,
The laughing and dancing,
All the animals there.

But at bedtime I ran
As quick as could be
To fall asleep dreaming
Of my gorilla and me.

The End

CPSIA information can be obtained
at www.ICGtesting.com
Printed in the USA
BVHW021934020919
557385BV00012B/156/P